ALI BABA AND THE FORTY THIEVES

RETOLD FROM THE ORIGINAL BY ANTOINE GALLAND

Once upon a time in Persia lived two brothers, Kassim and Ali Baba. Kassim was married to a wealthy woman and was a very rich merchant. Ali Baba was just a simple woodcutter, and had married a woman as poor as himself.

One day, Ali Baba was collecting wood in the forest, when he noticed a group of strange men on horseback.

"Robbers," Ali Baba thought to himself. "They must have a hideout near here. I'd better hide in this tree."

From his perch Ali Baba counted forty men: all armed. Their leader rode up to a huge rock, and commanded: "Open Sesame!" With these words, the rock rolled back and the robbers disappeared into a large cave.

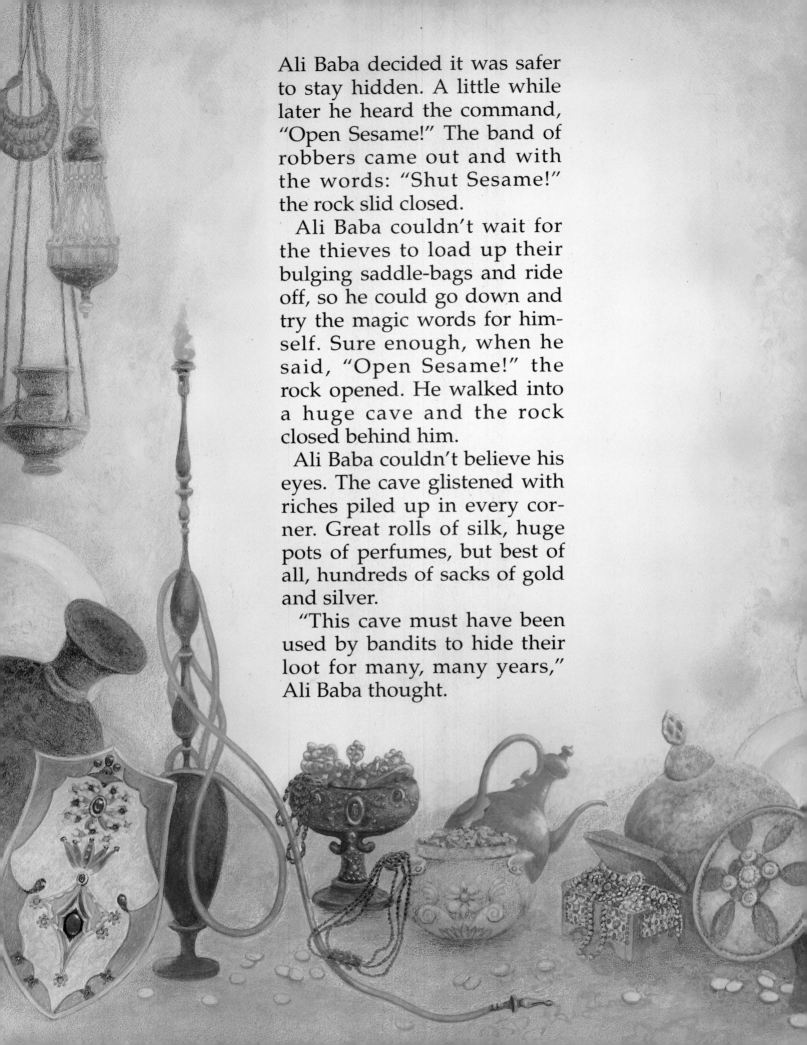

Ali Baba decided it was safer to stay hidden. A little while later he heard the command, "Open Sesame!" The band of robbers came out and with the words: "Shut Sesame!" the rock slid closed.

Ali Baba couldn't wait for the thieves to load up their bulging saddle-bags and ride off, so he could go down and try the magic words for himself. Sure enough, when he said, "Open Sesame!" the rock opened. He walked into a huge cave and the rock closed behind him.

Ali Baba couldn't believe his eyes. The cave glistened with riches piled up in every corner. Great rolls of silk, huge pots of perfumes, but best of all, hundreds of sacks of gold and silver.

"This cave must have been used by bandits to hide their loot for many, many years," Ali Baba thought.

He decided to take as many bags of gold as his donkeys could carry. "Open Sesame!" he commanded, then when he was outside, "Shut Sesame!" and the rock rolled back. He loaded up the gold, disguising his load with the wood he had cut, and made his way back into town. When he got home, he stealthily unloaded the sacks and took them in to his wife.

Ali Baba told her the whole story. She was delighted, and wanted to count the sacks of gold there and then.

"There are far too many," Ali Baba told her. "We must bury the gold, and keep the whole thing a secret."

"Let me just measure it," she pleaded, "so we have an idea of our riches."

So Ali Baba allowed her to go to his brother Kassim's wife to borrow a measuring jar. Kassim's wife was curious to know what such poor people could be measuring, so she dropped some sticky wax into the bottom of the jar.

When Ali Baba's wife had measured all the gold - which took quite some time as there was so much - she returned the jar. Kassim's wife was amazed when she found a gold coin stuck to the bottom.

She taunted Kassim: "You think you're rich, but your brother has so much gold his wife has to measure it rather than count it."

Kassim was very jealous and he rushed to Ali Baba and demanded to know the truth. Ali Baba was a kind man, so he decided to share his secret with his brother.

5

At first light, the greedy
Kassim set off for the cave,
taking with him ten mules on
which to load the gold. He
found the rock and with the
words, "Open Sesame!" he
was quickly inside.

He was so excited by the
riches he saw, that when he'd
filled his bags with gold and
was ready to go, he found he
had completely forgotten the
magic words. Try as he might
he couldn't get out.

Outside the cave the band of
forty thieves had returned
from their latest robbery.

Seeing Kassim's mules they became suspicious and drew their daggers and swords before their leader opened the cave with the magic words. Rushing inside they found the intruder and quickly finished him off.

The robbers couldn't think how the intruder had got in, but they decided to leave his body in the cave as a warning to anyone else who might know the secret words.

When Kassim didn't return, his wife ran to Ali Baba and confessed her husband's plan to take the gold. Next morning Ali Baba went to the cave.

"Open Sesame!" he cried, and the rock swung open to reveal his brother's body. Poor Kassim, his greed had been his downfall. Ali Baba wanted to give him a decent burial, but he had to be careful of the robbers.

Ali Baba returned to Kassim's house with the body. He took Morgiana, his brother's faithful servant aside, and after swearing her to secrecy, told her the story.

"Now," he said, "we must bury your master as if he died of a fever. I'm leaving all the details to you."

First Morgiana went to a doctor. "My master is ill," she told him. "Can you give me something for a fever?" Then she took the medicine home, so all the neighbours knew Kassim was ill.

Next she went to the shoemaker, Baba Mustapha. She told him: "For three gold coins, you must do a job for me, and keep it secret," and she led him blindfolded to Kassim's house.

When they arrived she explained that he must use his stitch skills to disguise the many wounds her master had received. When his task was complete he was blindfolded again and led home.

The next day, Ali Baba announced that Kassim had died. They laid his body in a fine coffin and there was a big public ceremony. No-one suspected anything.

Meanwhile, back at the robbers' cave, the bandits had returned to find the body of the intruder gone.

"There is someone else who knows the magic words to open this cave," the leader told his gang. "If we're not very careful, all our riches will be stolen away from under our very noses!"

He stopped to think. "One of you must go into town and discover who has buried a friend or relative who died in mysterious circumstances."

One of the band volunteered, and off he rode. He arrived just as the sun was going down and the first shop he came to was that of the shoemaker. Seeing the old man busy with his needle, the robber said, "You have good eyesight old man, to work in this poor light."

"Why yes," replied Baba Mustapha. "Only the other night I had to do a very delicate task in even less light."

The robber was curious and before long Baba Mustapha had told him all about sewing up Kassim's wounds.

"Believe me my friend," the robber said, "you will earn a lot more money, if you take me to the house where you performed this operation."

"I would like to help," Baba Mustapha told the robber, "but I was blindfolded when I was taken to the house."

But the robber was not to be put off. He persuaded Mustapha to let him blindfold him, then he led him across the town.

Sure enough, the route was familiar to the shoemaker, and directly outside Kassim's house he stopped and told

the robber, "This is it, I feel certain that I went no further than this."

The robber was jubilant. His task had been easy. He carefully marked the door that Baba Mustapha had recognised with a cross, then hurried back to inform his chief. They would do away with the people who lived at that house, and the secret of the rock would again be safe.

Luckily for Ali Baba - who was now living in Kassim's house - Morgiana returned from an errand just at this moment. She noticed the cross on the door of the house and thought to herself, "What is this mark? I wouldn't be surprised if it has been made by someone who wishes to do harm to my new master."

She then came up with a very clever idea to protect Ali Baba and his family. Morgiana went around all

the houses in the street and marked their doors with an identical cross to the one on the front of her own door.

When the gang of robbers arrived later that night, they were thrown into total confusion. There were crosses on all the doors in the neighbourhood, and the robber who had marked Kassim's door had no idea which was the correct house. The leader of the gang was so furious that he killed the unsuccessful robber on the spot.

The gang returned to the cave, and another robber volunteered to lead the shoemaker to the intruder's door.

Baba Mustapha was happy to repeat his trip, for a few gold coins. When he had identified the house, the robber marked the door with a lump of red clay. He was sure his plan would succeed.

Luckily, Morgiana was again keeping a watchful eye on things, and she spotted the red clay almost straight away. So she mixed herself a quantity of red clay, and again she marked all the other doors in the neighbourhood in exactly the same way.

You can imagine the fury of the robbers', and especially their chief, when they realized that yet again their plot had been discovered. And, unfortunately, their second guide was finished off in the same way as the first.

The robber chief now decided to take matters into his own hands. He went into town and had Baba Mustapha lead him to Kassim's house. He then memorized exactly where it was. When he returned to the cave, he gave orders for his men to obtain nineteen mules and thirty-eight large jars for carrying oil.

Then the chief hid one thief in each of thirty-seven of the jars, putting the tops on with just enough room for air to get in. He then filled the final jar with oil, disguised himself as an oil seller and set off for town. He arrived at Ali Baba's house just as the sun was going down, and explained he was a travelling merchant needing a room for the night. Ali Baba was such a generous man, he naturally offered his own home.

Although Ali Baba had seen the robber chief at the cave, he didn't recognise him because of his disguise. So he allowed him to stable his mules and stack the oil jars, before entertaining him with food and drink.

Before going to bed, the chief visited the courtyard where the jars were stacked. He whispered to each one: "When I throw stones, climb out and wait for me."

Meanwhile, Morgiana was busy in the kitchen. When her lamp ran out of oil, she remembered all the jars, and decided to borrow some oil. As she approached she heard a whisper from one of the jars, "Is it time?"

She was astounded, but realized there was something suspicious going on. "Not yet, but soon," she whispered back. Then she tried the remaining jars and had the same response from all but the last, which contained oil.

"Good heavens," thought Morgiana. "Thirty-seven thieves in my master's house, and their chief asleep upstairs, what am I to do?"

Naturally, she came up with a plan. She took a large pan and filled it with oil from the last jar, then she heated it over a fire. Returning to the jars, she poured just enough oil into each jar to kill the thief hiding there.

Later the robber chief began throwing stones at the jars. When nothing happened, he crept downstairs to see what the problem was. Finding his whole band of robbers had been killed, he fled from the house in dismay.

When Ali Baba woke the next day, Morgiana explained the night's events to him. "Master," she finished, "I beg of you, be on your guard."

They buried the pots and their grisly contents at the bottom of the garden. And to show his gratitude, Ali Baba gave Morgiana her freedom.

Meanwhile the robber chief was plotting his revenge. He bought a house close by and, wearing a new disguise, introduced himself to Ali Baba as a wealthy merchant.

One evening, Ali Baba and his son invited their new neighbour to dinner. The robber came armed with a dagger. Luckily, Morgiana was as alert as ever, and recognised the thief, even through his disguise. After dinner, she dressed as a dancer and entertained the guest.

At the most exciting moment of the dance, she rushed forward and stabbed the chief through the heart. Ali Baba was horrified: "You have brought dishonour to my house," he cried.

Morgiana revealed the chief's dagger, and replied, "This is none other than the chief of thieves."

Ali Baba was so overcome with gratitude, that he begged Morgiana to honour him by agreeing to marry his son. Naturally she agreed.